Einstein Anderson Shocks His Friends

EINSTEIN ANDERSON

Shocks His Friends

Seymour Simon

Illustrated by Fred Winkowski

The Viking Press, New York

For Linda Zuckerman,
with friendship and affection

First Edition
Text Copyright © Seymour Simon, 1980
Illustrations Copyright © The Viking Press, 1980
All rights reserved
First published in 1980 by The Viking Press
625 Madison Avenue, New York, New York 10022
Published simultaneously in Canada by Penguin Books Canada Limited
Printed in U.S.A.
1   2   3   4   5   84   83   82   81   80

Library of Congress Cataloging in Publication Data
Simon, Seymour.   Einstein Anderson shocks his friends.
(Einstein Anderson, science sleuth; 2)
Summary: Einstein Anderson uses his scientific
knowledge to solve a variety of problems, including
getting rid of a bully and preserving a snow sculpture.
[1. Science—Problems, exercises, etc.—Fiction]
I. Winkowski, Fred. II. Title. III. Series:
Simon, Seymour. Einstein Anderson, science sleuth; 2.
PZ7.S60573EK   [Fic]   80–15786   ISBN 0–670–29070–x

Contents

In this book, Einstein Anderson solves puzzles by using his knowledge in these areas of science:

electricity

zoology

radioactivity

biology

motion

space science

chemistry

heat

change of state

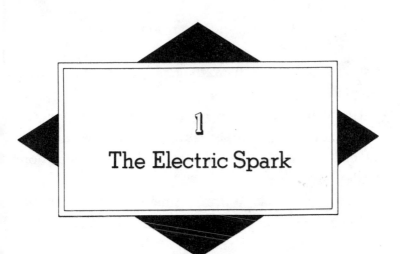

1
The Electric Spark

The alarm clock started to ring just as Einstein Anderson was pulling the bedcovers around him more comfortably. Einstein drowsily looked around his bedroom. He couldn't remember why he had set the alarm for so early in the morning. Was he going to the beach? Was there a ball game today? Were there some experiments he wanted to do?

Then Einstein remembered. Today was the first day of school in the town of Sparta. Summer vacation was over. Sleeping late in the mornings (except on weekends) was a thing of the past. Today was his first day in sixth grade, in Sparta Middle School.

He would just have to get up and shut off the alarm, Einstein thought. But instead of getting out of bed, he snuggled down for a few seconds more under the covers.

"Shut off that alarm, Einstein," his younger brother, Dennis, called out from his bedroom. "I can't stand that noise."

It was also the first day of school for Dennis. He was going into third grade in Sparta Elementary School. But he didn't have his own alarm clock. He didn't need one. Einstein always made sure he woke up Dennis on schooldays. It was a pleasure.

"Adam, Dennis, are you boys getting up? Breakfast will be ready in ten minutes," Mrs. Anderson called from downstairs.

Adam was Einstein's real name. But most people called him Einstein, after the most famous scientist of the twentieth century. Adam had been interested in science for as long as he could remember. He had solved so many science puzzles that his friends and even some of his teachers began to call him by the nickname of Einstein.

"I'm getting up now," Einstein called back. He got out of bed and went over to his dresser to shut off the alarm clock. Einstein kept the alarm out of reach from his bed because he knew that otherwise he would just shut it off and go back to sleep. From next door he heard Dennis getting out of bed, still grumbling about the noisy alarm clock.

Einstein went into the bathroom and washed. He came back to his room and looked out the window. It was a dry, cool day in early September, with a hint of autumn in the air.

Einstein decided to wear a long-sleeve shirt, jeans, sneakers, and his nylon baseball jacket. The jeans were Einstein's favorite pair, all raggedy at the knees. But just as he was about to put them on, he remembered that his mother had insisted that he wear a new pair for the first day of school.

The new jeans were stiff and didn't feel right. Einstein sighed as he got into them. Who knows why parents have this thing about wearing new clothing on the first day of school? he thought.

Dr. Anderson, Einstein's father, was making coffee when Einstein and Dennis came down for breakfast. He greeted the boys with affection. Dr. Anderson was a veterinarian. He was often out on emergency calls even before his sons got up in the morning.

Mrs. Anderson was just putting a big stack of pancakes onto a plate. She poured a glassful of juice for each of the boys. Then she accepted a cupful of coffee from her husband.

"Mom, which hand do you use to stir your coffee?" asked Einstein.

"Why, my right hand," said Mrs. Anderson, looking surprised at the question.

"That's funny," said Einstein. "Most people stir their coffee with a spoon."

Everybody groaned. Einstein loved to tell jokes, the worse the better.

"Just finish up quickly," said Mrs. Anderson. "I have to get down to the office, and I don't have time to listen to bad jokes," she said amiably. Mrs. Anderson worked as a writer and editor on the Sparta *Tribune*, one of the town's two newspapers. She often used the things her boys said and did in humorous stories she wrote for the paper.

Einstein and Dennis finished breakfast and promised to clean the dishes when they got home from school. Then they took pens and notebooks and left the house.

On the way to the school bus stop Einstein showed his brother a rock he had found the day before. It had glittery flakes and was called mica schist. He also pointed out a large click beetle on the ground.

"Why is it called a click beetle?" Dennis asked.

"This is why," Einstein answered. He turned the beetle over on its back. The beetle lay quietly for a moment. Then, with a loud click, it flipped into the air and landed on its feet. In an instant it scurried away.

There were only a few children on the bus when it rolled up at the stop near the Andersons' house. When Einstein got on the bus, he saw that Pat Burns was sitting near the back.

Pat Burns was not one of Einstein's favorite people. In fact, Pat Burns was Einstein's least favorite classmate. Everyone in the class called him Pat the Brat. Pat was the biggest kid in the class and also the meanest. He was always trying to play tricks on other kids. Einstein would stand up to Pat when he had to, but he usually tried to handle Pat by outthinking him.

Einstein was just about to duck down into a seat near the front door when Pat called out. "Well, well. Look who's there. If it isn't my famous classmate, Einstein Anderson. And there's his baby brother, Dennis."

"Who are you calling a baby?" Dennis said. "If you want to see what a baby looks like, why don't you look in a mirror?"

"What's that?" Pat said. "You trying to pick a fight with me? You'll fall down if I blow on you."

"With breath like yours, a lot of people would fall down," Dennis said.

Einstein began to laugh, but stopped when he saw Pat making his way to the front of the bus. Pat stood in front of Einstein and spoke to him. "Can you think of any reason why I shouldn't punch you now?" he asked.

"I can't think of any reason why you should," Einstein said. "And I can think of several reasons why you shouldn't."

"Name one," Pat said.

"One reason is that I'll punch you back," Einstein said. "And another reason is that you can never tell what will happen when you punch a scientist."

"I'll take my chances," Pat said.

Einstein looked thoughtful. Would he have to fight Pat? His glasses slipped down over his nose, and he pushed them back with his finger. Suddenly he stood up. He pulled up the sleeves of his jacket. Then he rapidly began to pump his arms back and forth alongside his body as if he were running in a race.

"What are you doing?" asked Pat. "Are you going crazy?"

"Not a bit," said Einstein. "I just want you to see I have nothing up my sleeve. I'm about to give you the shock of your life."

Einstein brought up his arm and pointed his finger at Pat's nose. Suddenly a spark snapped from the tip of Einstein's finger to the tip of Pat's nose. Pat yelled and staggered back. In an instant he was in the back of the bus, trying to get as far away as possible from Einstein.

"That was great," Dennis said. "You came to school all wired up?"

"No," said Einstein. "I just knew it was a good day for a spark."

Can you solve the puzzle: How did Einstein make the spark?

The bus began to fill up with people. Over the noisy conversations all around them Dennis asked, "Is that really an electric spark?"

"Yes," Einstein said. "There's really a very simple explanation. I could make a spark because of static electricity."

"So you *are* wired for electricity," Dennis said.

"It has nothing to do with wires," Einstein said. "All kinds of things contain electrical charges, positive and negative. Normally there are equal amounts of positive and negative charges, so they cancel each other out. You don't feel anything."

"You mean that I have electricity in me?" asked Dennis, pointing to himself.

"We all do," Einstein said. "So do all kinds of materials—including nylon and wool. But you can make the electricity move by rubbing. You know the way you sometimes use a nylon comb to comb your hair and you hear it crackle? Or when you take off a woolen sweater and you get sparks? Well, that's what just happened. When I rubbed my arms against my nylon jacket, I became charged with electricity. I put my finger near Pat's nose, and the electrical charge jumped from my hand to his nose. I could have done the same thing if I'd been standing on a wool or nylon rug and rubbed my feet against it." He shuffled his feet back and forth on the floor of the bus.

"So the day had nothing to do with the spark?" Dennis asked.

"Yes, it did," Einstein said. "If the air were humid, the electrical charge would leak off quickly and there would be no sparks. But today is cold and dry, a perfect day for static electricity."

"Well, that static electricity certainly took care of Pat," Dennis said with a satisfied smile.

"Right," Einstein said. "I'm sure he got a charge out of it."

2
The Strange Pet

"You know that I just don't like keeping the usual kinds of pets, Einstein," Stanley said. He brushed back his long black hair, which was falling into his eyes.

"You mean like your baby boa constrictor?" Einstein asked. "Or like the carpenter ant nest you keep in your basement?"

"No. They're just the regular kinds of pets," Stanley said. "I mean something really unusual. Something that you just won't believe I've been lucky enough to get."

"Don't tell me, let me guess," Einstein said.

Stanley Roberts was a teenaged friend of Einstein's, just as interested in science as Einstein was. The boys were talking in Stanley's "laboratory"—an attic room Stanley's parents had let him use for his experiments. The room was overflowing with what looked like junk . . . but what Stanley said was "scientific apparatus."

"You're going to get a king cobra, the deadliest snake in the world," said Einstein, who enjoyed kidding Stanley. "Or maybe a great white shark just like in *Jaws.* No? Then are you going to get the animal that never plays fair?"

"What animal is that?" Stanley asked, despite the fact that he was shaking his head back and forth to every animal Einstein had named.

"An animal that never plays fair," Einstein said, "is obviously a cheetah."

Stanley groaned. "I never should have asked," he said. "Stop kidding around, Einstein. I'm serious. Do you want me to tell you what animal I'm getting or do you just want to hear about it on the news?"

"Sorry," Einstein said. "Please tell me. As the corn plant said, I'm all ears."

"Good," Stanley said. "Now listen to this. A few weeks ago I saw an advertisement in a magazine for a unique pet. Something that no one in this

country has. Of course, it's only a baby because it would be impossible to keep a full-grown one in your home."

"That really does sound interesting," Einstein said. "Don't keep me in suspense. What's the name of the animal?"

"The advertisement just called it an LNM. They said it comes from a very deep lake in the northern part of the British Isles."

"What does it look like?" Einstein asked.

"I wrote to the people in the ad and they sent back a description of the pet. It's green and has a scaly skin. It has a long neck and flippers and is a very good swimmer."

"How big is it?" Einstein asked.

"Well, this one is just a baby, so it will go in that fifty-gallon aquarium I have in the basement," Stanley said.

"What are you going to do when it outgrows the aquarium?"

"I'm going to make a special arrangement with the State Public Aquarium. They're sure to take it because no one else has anything like it. I wouldn't be surprised if the newspapers and TV make a big thing of my giving the LNM to the Public Aquarium. Maybe your mother would like to write an article about it for her paper, Einstein." He brushed back his hair and looked pleased with himself.

"Maybe," Einstein said. His glasses were slipping off the end of his nose. You could tell he was thinking.

"What's the matter? You don't look too happy," Stanley said.

"I'm not sure," Einstein said, "but I have the feeling that there's something familiar about your pet. Tell me, Stanley, is the pet expensive?"

"It sure is," Stanley said. "I had to work at odd jobs for weeks to be able to afford the money. You see, the people selling the pet had to get an export license from Scotland to be able to send it out of the country."

"From Scotland! Oh, no!" exclaimed Einstein. "Did you send the money yet?"

"Not yet," Stanley said. "I thought I'd go down to the post office and buy a money order to send in the mail. That way the money won't get lost."

"I have a better way to prevent you from losing the money," Einstein said.

"What's that?" Stanley asked.

"Don't send it," said Einstein.

Can you solve the puzzle: What is the strange pet? Why shouldn't Stanley send for it?

"Why?" Stanley asked. "Do you think there's something fishy going on?"

"Fishy is not exactly the word I would use," said Einstein. "Monstrous would be more like it."

"What are you talking about, Einstein? What do you think the pet is?"

"Let's look at the clues, Stanley. First, there are the initials LNM. Second is that it comes from a very deep lake in Scotland. Third is that it is green, has a long neck, and is a good swimmer."

"I still don't get it," said Stanley.

"I'll give you one more hint," Einstein said. "The Scottish word for lake is loch. The L in LNM stands for a particular loch."

Stanley's face started to turn red. "Oh, no," he said. "If L stands for Loch, then N must stand for Ness . . ."

"And M stands for Monster," finished Einstein. "The advertisement was for a baby Loch Ness Monster. Even if such an animal exists, it has never been caught. The people who wrote the advertisement were just trying to cheat anyone silly enough to send in money."

"I guess you're right, Einstein," Stanley said. He looked glum.

Einstein tried to cheer him up. "Don't be depressed," he said. "After all, it was your scientific curiosity that made you want to send for the LNM."

"I guess. But maybe skepticism would have been better."

Einstein picked up a magazine lying on a table and flipped through the pages. "It's true," he said. "Look at some of these stories. Here's one about someone sighting a UFO and meeting the aliens when they came out of the spaceship. Here's an article that tells you if it's your lucky day because of the position of the stars and the planets. A scientist needs proof before he believes everything he reads or hears."

"Well, I feel like a fool for talking myself into sending for a baby Loch Ness Monster," Stanley said.

Einstein couldn't resist. "You weren't a fool for talking to yourself," he said. "Only for listening."

3

Relics of the
Lost Continent

Today was the first Saturday since school had opened. Einstein had wanted to sleep late in the morning, but Margaret had asked him to visit and spend the day at her house.

In the morning they planned to work on a science project they were doing for school. The experiment involved the use of a Geiger counter. Margaret had borrowed the counter from her Aunt Bess, who was a professor of biology at State University. After they worked on their project Margaret was going to show Einstein her new discovery.

Margaret Michaels was a classmate and good friend of Einstein. She was also his rival for the title of best science student in the school. She was always trying to trick him with some science puzzle or other. Usually Einstein was able to solve the puzzles, but he knew Margaret was determined to stump him.

When Einstein arrived at Margaret's house, the Geiger counter was set up on a table along with the other materials needed for the project.

"You know that a Geiger counter flashes a light and clicks when radioactivity is present," Margaret said.

"Sure, the more flashes of light and the quicker the clicks, the greater the radioactivity," Einstein said.

"That's right," said Margaret. She pointed to a meter on the counter. "You can read the amount of radioactivity right from this meter. Now let's go over the plans for the project we're working on for the science fair. We're going to experiment to find out whether a fertilizer placed in the soil really is used by a plant. We're going to test for a chemical in fertilizer called phosphorus. Aunt Bess is getting some radioactive phosphorus for her laboratory at the university. She wants us to set up two groups of coleus plants for our tests. She'll pick up the plants tonight and put the radiophosphorus in the soil on Monday."

"Then we can test to see if any of the phosphorus gets into the leaves of the coleus," Einstein said.

"That's right," said Margaret. "We'll go to visit Bess next weekend. Then she'll show us how we can use the counter to safely test the leaves of the plants to see if they contain radioactivity."

"If they do, that will show that the leaves picked up the radiophosphorus from the soil," Einstein said. "It sounds like a good project for the fair."

"It is," Margaret said. "Now let's get to work with the plants."

For the next hour Margaret and Einstein planted and matched in size and healthy appearance coleus plants in four pots. Finally they were finished with their task.

"Let's eat lunch first," Margaret said. "Then I'm going to show you some of my secret findings that will stun the world of science. I bet I'll get a prize for these discoveries. Wait till you see what I've found."

Einstein was bubbling over with curiosity, but he decided to play it cool. "Sure, Margaret," he said, "you'll get a prize . . . but I won't hold my breath until you do. Let's eat."

After lunch Margaret led Einstein back to the table with the Geiger counter. She motioned him to be seated and then went out of the room. When she returned, she had a cardboard box in her hands.

"Before I show you the strange objects in this box," Margaret said, "I have to tell you something about Atlantis. Have you ever heard of Atlantis, Einstein?"

Einstein looked at the box Margaret had brought into the room. What connection could the box have with Atlantis? he wondered.

"You mean the so-called lost continent of Atlantis?" he asked. "That was a continent that was supposed to exist centuries ago. Then something happened, maybe an earthquake or a volcano, and the land was completely destroyed. But isn't that just a myth?"

"Maybe not." Margaret's face lit up with enthusiasm as she went on. "Atlantis was supposed to have sunk below the waves. For hundreds of years people have searched for the lost city. But now I think I have found proof that it really exists."

Margaret emptied the cardboard box on the table. "Look at these things," she said.

Einstein went over to the table and looked down at two objects. One was a dagger that was made of a yellowish metal. The other was a thin sheet of what looked like paper with some kind of writing covering one side.

"It doesn't look like much to me," Einstein said. "Just a brass knife and a piece of some kind of paper with chicken tracks on it."

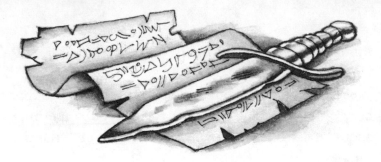

"Those chicken tracks are really the secret writings of the Elders of Atlantis," Margaret said. "I found these things in an old sea chest in the attic. It must have been there since the house was built before we lived here." She pointed to the paper. "By carefully working on the writing I was able to find out that it comes from the lost island of Atlantis."

"Do you expect me to believe that?" asked Einstein. "Do I look like Pat the Brat? I bet you just made these up to fool me. What proof do you have that these things are really centuries old?"

"The scientific proof of radioactivity," said Margaret. "You know that the age of certain objects can be told by the amount of radioactivity in them."

"Sure I know," said Einstein. "Like radioactive carbon dating."

"That's just what I used," said Margaret. "Radioactive carbon is called carbon 14. Carbon 14 is found in objects made from plant and animal materials. The amount of carbon 14 decreases at the rate of one-half every 5570 years. For example, if a piece of wood is found to have half the carbon of a tree living today, its age is thought to be 5570 years old."

"And you used the Geiger counter to date these objects?" asked Einstein.

"Exactly," said Margaret. "It is my estimate that the dagger and paper are more than five thousand years old."

"Come on, Margaret," said Einstein. "You know that carbon 14 dating is very difficult. It has to be done with exact measurements in a laboratory. You mean that you just used this Geiger counter?"

"Can you prove that I didn't?" asked Margaret with a big smile. "If you can't prove I'm wrong, then I just may be right. And these things just may be the most important scientific discovery ever found by someone in the Sparta Middle School. What do you say to that, Einstein Anderson?"

Einstein was quiet for a minute. Then he pushed back his glasses, which were slipping down, and said, "I say that you forgot one very important fact, Margaret. And that fact proves that your story is as phony as the dagger and the paper."

Can you solve the puzzle: What was Margaret's mistake? How did Einstein know that her story was not true?

"I'm waiting, Einstein. What did I forget?" asked Margaret.

"You said yourself that carbon 14 dating can only be used on objects that were once living animals or plants," said Einstein.

"Uh-oh," said Margaret. "I think I know what I did wrong. It's the dagger, isn't it?"

"Yep. It's the dagger that gave you away. The dagger is made of metal, not an animal or a plant. And anything made of metal can never be dated by carbon 14."

"I'll fool you next time," Margaret said as she gathered up her things.

"First you better get advice from a builder," said Einstein.

"Why a builder?" Margaret asked.

"Because he'll tell you if you're going to construct stories—"

"Yes?"

"—you need a good foundation."

4

The Halloween Horror

Halloween was the best time to see a good ghost movie. That's what Dennis Anderson kept on telling his mother. Finally Mrs. Anderson agreed. Dennis could go to the Saturday matinee to see *The Halloween Horror* if Einstein would take him.

"That's swell, Mom," Dennis said. "I'll ask Einstein now. He loves science fiction and monster movies, so I'm sure he'll want to go."

Dennis ran up the stairs to Einstein's room and flung open the door. Einstein was lying on the bed reading a book about the time senses of living things.

"Mom said I could go to see *The Halloween Horror* if you take me. How about it, Einstein? Please?" said Dennis.

"I wish you'd learn how to knock on a door before you come in," said Einstein, looking up from his book. "Suppose I was working on an experiment and you burst in."

"Sorry," Dennis said. "Will you take me to see the movie? We can make the two o'clock show on Saturday."

Einstein thought for a minute. "That'll be O.K., Dennis," he said. "I have to go over to Margaret's house to work on a project in the morning, but I'll be back for lunch and then we can go to see *The Halloween Horror.*"

Saturday was a bright, sunny day. Einstein got up early and went over to Margaret's house. Dennis went out to have a catch with a friend. They both came back at noon, had lunch, and set out for the movie.

Along the way Einstein pointed out to Dennis that a shadow was shorter at noon than early in the morning or late in the afternoon. He explained how a sundial worked and how it was the earth that turned each day to make the sun appear to rise and set. He also began to explain how the sun's heating causes wind, but he suddenly stopped.

"I just remembered something," Einstein said. "Dennis, do you know what colors you would paint the sun and the wind?"

"No. What?" Dennis said.

"You would paint the sun rose and the wind blue," said Einstein.

"Ugh," Dennis said. "Stick to the science part, Einstein. Or let's talk about the ghost movie we're going to see."

"Talking about ghosts," Einstein said, "do you know how a ghost opens a door?"

"How?"

"With a skeleton key," Einstein said.

"That's terrible," said Dennis.

"Yeah, I guess I just have to re-*hearse* my ghost jokes some more," Einstein said.

"I give up," Dennis said.

There was a line at the box office when the boys arrived at the movie theater. Einstein finally purchased their tickets and the boys went inside.

The movie hadn't begun yet, but the theater was quite dark. Einstein bought a box of popcorn, and he and Dennis made their way to seats near the front.

As soon as they sat down, a voice called out to them from the back of the theater. "Einstein, it's me, Pat. Herman is here with me. Can we sit with you and your brother? We're coming over now."

Einstein slunk down in his seat. Why would Pat want to sit with him? They had hardly been on speaking terms after Einstein had shocked Pat on the bus the first day of school. And Einstein wasn't much friendlier with Herman, Pat's sidekick.

"How are you, Einstein old buddy?" Pat said. "Herman and me just came into the movie, and when I saw you sitting here I just knew you'd want us to sit with you. Right, Herman?"

"Whatever you say, Pat," Herman said in a puzzled way. "But what about the wa—"

"Never mind, Herman," Pat exclaimed. "Just keep your mouth shut and let me do the thinking."

"That's asking the impossible. Both ways," Einstein said.

Before Pat could reply, an usher ran over to where Pat and Herman were sitting. "You're the boys who threw the water bomb from the balcony," he said. "You got a whole bunch of second-grade kids wet. Now they'll have to go home to change and they'll miss the movie. So I'm throwing you two out of the theater."

"Why us?" Pat said. "We never threw nothing.

When did all this happen? We just came into the movie, and we saw our friend Einstein here and came over to sit next to him." Pat turned to Einstein. "Ain't that right?" he said.

"Well, you did just come over here," said Einstein. He looked thoughtful. "When did the kids get hit?" he asked the usher.

"About ten minutes ago," said the usher. "I was trying to take care of them till now. But I spotted the boys who threw the water bomb, and I think these two are the ones."

"How could we have thrown the water bomb?" asked Pat. "I told you we just came into the movie."

Einstein pushed his glasses back on his nose. "Throwing a water bomb on young kids is no joke," he said. "Now they can't see the movie, and I think the ones who threw the water bomb shouldn't see it either."

"But we just came in," Pat said. "So it couldn't be us."

"That's not true, Pat," Einstein said. "You didn't just come in. You've been here for quite a while."

Can you solve the puzzle: How did Einstein know that Pat and Herman had not just come into the theater?

"Oh, yeah?" said Pat. "How do you know how long we've been here? You just came in yourself."

"That's just it," Einstein said. "I just came in and I still can't see too well. It's bright sunshine outside and very dark in here. It takes at least ten or fifteen minutes for anyone's eyes to get adjusted to the dark so they can see anything."

"So what?" Pat asked.

"So how come you were able to recognize me from the back of the theater? If you had just come in, you wouldn't even have been able to see me if I was sitting in the back row, much less the front."

"Let's go," said the usher to Pat and Herman. "Out, out! I knew I saw you two drop the water bomb."

Einstein turned to Dennis as Pat and Herman were being led away. "You know," he said, "maybe Pat *was* able to see as soon as he came in. After all, he's usually in the dark."

5
The Broken Window

Einstein was eager to get to school before class began to talk to Margaret about their science project. He called Margaret the night before to make plans. They arranged to meet in the school yard at eight the next morning.

Einstein got up early. He washed, dressed, and went down to make himself breakfast. His father was sitting in the kitchen drinking a cup of coffee and reading the morning newspaper.

"What are you doing up so early in the morning, Adam?" Dr. Anderson asked. Einstein's father and mother still called their son by his real name.

"I'm going to school early today to meet Margaret to go over our project," Einstein answered.

"That's good," Dr. Anderson said. "Getting up early is one way you can get ahead."

"No, thank you, Dad," said Einstein. "I've already got one."

Dr. Anderson groaned. "No more, Adam," he said. "It's too early in the morning for puns."

Einstein didn't agree with his father. It was never too early—or too late—for a good joke, he thought. But the look on his father's face convinced him that now was not the time to argue the point. So he finished breakfast rapidly, got his jacket, and went out to catch the early bus to school.

The bus was supposed to make a pickup at seven-thirty. But seven-thirty came and went and the bus didn't show up. It was too late to make his eight o'clock appointment if he started walking. Einstein was just about to go back to his house and ask his father for a lift to school when he saw the bus coming.

When the bus drew up at the stop, Einstein could see that there was something wrong. The rear window of the bus was broken and there was glass all over the back ledge.

Einstein boarded the bus and saw that the only passengers were two high school boys sitting in the

middle of the bus. They were talking together loudly and laughing at something.

One called out as he saw Einstein, "Hey, here's a four-eyed creep from baby school. Why is he getting on this bus? The baby school bus doesn't come till later."

Einstein began to get angry but didn't say anything. Discretion is the better part of valor, his father always said. Better not say anything or you might get punched was Einstein's way of putting it.

Einstein sat down in the seat just behind the driver. When the bus started, he leaned forward and asked, "What happened to the back window? Did you have an accident?"

"It might have been an accident," the driver said. He seemed very concerned. He pushed his cap back and continued, "And then again it might not have been."

"What do you mean?" asked Einstein. "Didn't you see how it happened? Isn't the broken window the reason the bus is late?"

"Well, the truth is that I really didn't see how the window got broken. Those high school boys were playing around in the back seat. Suddenly I heard a loud crash and I jammed on the brakes. I thought the bus had hit something. When I turned around the window was broken."

"Didn't the boys in the back see what happened?" Einstein asked.

"That's just it. They claim that the loud crash was from outside the bus. They say that when I jammed on the brakes they were flung backwards

against the window. One of the boys was holding his books. The books hit the window so hard that the glass broke."

"Do you believe them?" asked Einstein.

"I don't know," the bus driver said. "I cleaned up the glass and told them to sit away from the back window. That's why the bus was late. I think those kids were fooling around and broke the glass on purpose. But I can't prove it, so I'll just have to watch them more carefully in the future. They're always causing one kind of trouble or another on the bus."

Einstein pushed his glasses back and was quiet for a few minutes. "What would happen if you could prove that they broke the window and that their story was just a phony?" he asked.

"If they were responsible, then they'd have to pay for the glass by doing chores after school. And they'd be warned that if they fooled around so dangerously again, they'd have to walk to school rather than go on the bus. But how can I prove that they broke the window?"

"I think there is a way," said Einstein. "Ask them to come up here and repeat their story."

Can you solve the puzzle: How can Einstein prove that the boys are lying?

The bus driver stopped the bus and called the two high school boys to the front. "I want you to tell me how the window broke," he said.

"We already told you," one of the boys said.

"Tell me again," the bus driver said.

"I'll tell him," the other boy said. "It was like this. There was a crash from outside the bus. I guess the bus must have broken a bottle or something. Then you jammed on the brakes. I had these books in my hand and when the bus stopped so suddenly I fell backwards against the window. The books hit the window and broke it. It was an accident."

"That's impossible," Einstein said.

"What do you mean, impossible?" said the boy who told the story. "How do you know what happened? The only impossible thing is that you can prove I'm lying."

"Well, like the space scientists' motto says, the difficult we can do right away, the impossible takes a little longer. In your case, the impossible I can do right away."

"Prove it. All I hear is talk."

"The proof is simple. It just takes an understanding of inertia."

"What's that?" asked one of the boys.

"The law of inertia says that a body in motion tries to keep moving in the same direction," said Einstein. "When a bus stops suddenly, you and everything else fall toward the *front* of the bus, not toward the *back*. So you couldn't have broken the window by falling backwards into it. You broke the window in some other way, not because the bus stopped suddenly."

The boys looked at each other guiltily. "So we broke the window," one said. "What's it to you?

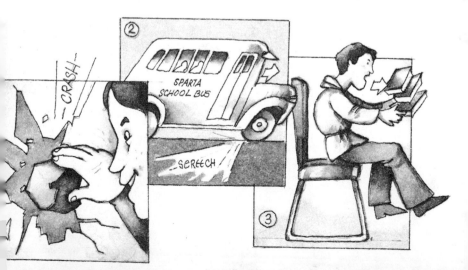

My dad will pay for the damage."

"You're not going to get off as easy as that," said the bus driver. "I'm sure that the principal, Mrs. Kaplan, will be interested to hear about you two troublemakers."

"Getting your parents to bail you out of trouble is what little kids would do," Einstein said.

"And I know just the kind of toy for kids like you," said the bus driver as he led them off. "A rattler."

6
The Science Test Papers

Ms. Taylor, Einstein's science teacher, was giving back yesterday's science test. As each student got back his test, everyone else in the class tried to get a peek at the mark. Usually it wasn't necessary. You could tell whether it was a good or a bad mark by the expression on the person's face.

Of course, no one would bother to look at Einstein's paper. He was sure to get all the answers right. But this time something odd happened.

Ms. Taylor stopped giving back the papers for an instant. "Children," she said, "I want to compliment Pat for turning in the best test paper in the class. He was the *only* one to get all the answers right." She gave Pat his paper.

The class started to buzz. Some turned to look at Pat, who was laughing and waving like a winner in a prize fight. Others turned to look at Einstein, who was shaking his head in surprise. Einstein couldn't remember any question on the test that he had found difficult. Which one had he gotten wrong? he wondered.

"Now here's your paper, Adam," said Ms. Taylor.
"I'm quite surprised at it. Perhaps you would like
to talk to me about it after class?"

Einstein took the paper and went back to his
seat. He looked at it with disbelief. It was covered
with crosses. The mark on the paper was 30. Was
that his paper? He looked at the name at the top.
Sure enough, the name at the top was Adam Anderson. And it was in his handwriting.

But wait a minute, Einstein said to himself. There were lots of erasures in the answers. He didn't remember making any erasures.

And what was this? He hadn't written "B" for the answer to the first question. He knew that the answer was "C," standing for Mars being called the red planet.

Not only that, but that "B" didn't even look like the way Einstein wrote a "B." The same thing was true of all the answers on Einstein's paper. All the wrong answers were not the ones he remembered writing. And underneath the wrong answers Einstein could see the original answers had been erased.

Einstein could barely wait to talk to Ms. Taylor about his paper. As soon as the class was dismissed for lunch, Einstein went up to his teacher's desk.

"Ms. Taylor," Einstein said, "there's something wrong with my test paper."

"I can see that," said Ms. Taylor. "I can't understand how you could have so many questions wrong. You've never gotten less than a hundred on any other science test."

"That's not what I mean," said Einstein. "The wrong answers on this paper are not the answers I wrote. Look at the way the letters are written. They're not in my handwriting. Not only that, but you can see that beneath the wrong answers, the original answers have been erased."

Ms. Taylor took the paper and looked at it closely. "You're right," she said. "I didn't notice the erasures when I was marking the test last night. But who could have made the changes, and how were they made?"

"The test was given yesterday morning," Einstein said. "Could you tell me what has happened to the papers since then?"

"Well, let's see," Ms. Taylor said. "I collected the papers and locked them away in my filing cabinet till three o'clock. I took them home last night to mark them. Then I brought them back today to give out to the class."

"Could anyone have gotten the key to the filing cabinet?" Einstein asked.

"I don't see how," Ms. Taylor said. "I have the key on a ring with my other school keys. I know that no one took the ring."

"Is there another key?" Einstein asked.

"I keep a spare key under a plant on top of the filing cabinet. I wonder if . . . you know I just remembered something. I sent Pat into the room to get some chalk yesterday. He took an awfully long time coming back. Do you think he could have taken the key?"

"Why don't we go in and look?" Einstein said.

"Let's go," said Ms. Taylor.

She led the way into her supply room down the hall from the classroom. The room was bright and sunny. The filing cabinet stood against one wall of the room. There was a landscape painting on the wall above the cabinet. A plant stood on top of the cabinet. Its broad leaves spilled toward the wall and touched the painting. There were also a desk and several chairs in the room. A large box of chalk and several packages of paper were on the desk.

"Does anything look like it's been disturbed?" Einstein asked.

"I'm not sure," Ms. Taylor said. "It seems to me that something is wrong, but I'm not sure what. Maybe it's just my imagination."

"What about the key?" asked Einstein. "Is it still under the plant?"

"I don't know," Ms. Taylor said. "I haven't

touched the plant since last Friday. Let me look."
She went over to the plant and lifted it off the filing
cabinet. Underneath the plant was the key.

"There's the key," Ms. Taylor said. "I suppose
Pat *could* have taken it, opened the cabinet,
changed the answers on the test papers, and then
returned the key. But how can I be sure?"

"Has anyone been in this room since Pat got the
chalk?" Einstein asked.

"No," said Ms. Taylor, "I'm positive that no one
has come into the room in the last week except
Pat and me."

"Then I'd like to ask Pat just one question,"
Einstein said. "If he answers that wrong, then
I'll know that he was the one who changed the
answers."

Can you solve the puzzle: What important clue
did Einstein notice? What question will he ask Pat?

Ms. Taylor sent a monitor to get Pat from the lunchroom. When Pat came into the supply room, he was no longer laughing.

"I suppose Einstein is complaining about his test mark," Pat said. "But what have I got to do with it?"

"We'll see," said Einstein. "Are you willing to answer one question so that we can be sure?"

"Why not?" Pat said. "I didn't do anything."

"When you came into the supply room yesterday to get chalk, did you touch anything else in the room?" asked Einstein.

"I didn't touch a thing except the chalk," Pat said.

"Are you sure that you didn't move the plant and take the key for the filing cabinet?" Einstein asked.

"I never touched the plant," Pat exclaimed.

"Then I know you're not telling the truth," Einstein said. "The leaves of a plant left alone grow toward the light. Yet the leaves on this plant are facing toward the wall, away from the sunlight. Someone picked up the plant and turned it around within the past day or two. Ms. Taylor hasn't touched the plant for a week, so the only one who could've turned the plant is you."

Pat's face sank. He looked worried.

"You must have found the key," Einstein continued, "opened the filing cabinet, changed your answers to those I had on my paper, and changed my answers to your old answers. Then you put the papers back in the cabinet, locked it, and replaced the key. The only trouble was that you put the plant back with the leaves facing the wrong way."

Einstein paused. Then, "You might say that this puzzle had a clue that was planted."

7
The Challenge of the Space Station

"The giant space station turned slowly high above Earth's atmosphere. From the approaching supply ship, the space station looked like an enormous bicycle wheel. The space station was to be the launching site for the first manned expedition to the planet Mars.

"How does that sound as an opening to our radio play, Einstein?" Margaret asked. "You know we're supposed to have the play written before Thanksgiving. Then we'll give out the parts and perform the play the week before the Christmas holidays."

"I'm not much good at writing," said Einstein. "I think I'd be better as a sort of technical adviser to make sure that all the science is accurate. If I wrote the play, then we would have a double celebration for Thanksgiving."

"What do you mean by a double celebration?" Margaret asked.

"The first would be a real turkey and the second would be a play that's a turkey."

"Cut out the jokes, Einstein," Margaret said, unable to suppress a smile. "I need your help to write the play, not to help me with the science part."

"I'm not so sure about that, Margaret," Einstein said. "I've been looking over the script you've written so far, and I think there are a number of places where the science is questionable."

"O.K., let's go over the places and make sure that the science is right and then we can get back to finishing the script. I hope you notice that I said *we*, Einstein."

"We'll talk about that later," Einstein said. "First, let's get the science part right."

"I'm waiting," said Margaret. "I don't think there's anything wrong. But I'm willing to discuss it with you."

"Right," Einstein said hastily, noticing a certain angry look beginning to appear in Margaret's eyes.

"In the script there are men and women working to finish the space station to get ready for the launch. The workers are in pressurized space suits to protect themselves from the lack of air in space. Of course, they are in a condition of zero gravity while orbiting Earth."

"Is there anything wrong with that?" Margaret asked.

"No, no," Einstein said. "I'm just going over the conditions so that we can agree about them."

"Go on," said Margaret.

"Well, here are some of the things that happen in the script," Einstein said. "You have the space station workers moving large girders easily by hand and swinging them into place. Some workers are using weightless hammers to drive in bolts. You also have a worker being hit by a weightless girder and not being hurt because it is weightless."

"So?" Margaret asked.

"Let me go on," Einstein said. "You have some other situations that happen later on. You have a space worker accidentally tearing a hole in his suit and then exploding because of the pressure in his body and the lack of any air in space."

"You still haven't told me anything that you think is wrong," Margaret said.

"When the electricity fails in the space station

and the lights go out, you have one of the characters light a candle so that he can see how to repair the generator," Einstein continued.

"Ah-ha," Margaret said. "I've got you there. The part of the space station where the candle was lit is pressurized and contains air. You don't think I'd have someone lighting a candle in a space vacuum, do you?"

"That's not it," said Einstein, "but the candle still wouldn't burn for long."

"But the space station has plenty of reserve air," said Margaret. "Why should it go out? Are there any errors at all in the script? It seems to me that everything you mentioned is correct."

"I don't think so," said Einstein. "There are four errors that I've spotted just in the situations I've gone over."

Can you solve the puzzle: What are the four errors that Einstein has spotted?

"Einstein," Margaret said, "if you can convince me that there are four errors, I'll write the rest of the script with you as the technical consultant."

"Terrific," said Einstein. "The first error I noticed is that the space station workers are moving large girders easily."

"But the girders are weightless in orbit," Margaret said.

"That's true, but it makes no difference in this case. The reason is that an object in motion tends to remain in motion and an object at rest tends to remain at rest."

"That's inertia," Margaret said.

"Right," Einstein continued. "The more matter in an object, the more inertia it has. Even in orbit the matter in an object remains the same, and so does its inertia. Large girders contain a lot of matter, so they are hard to move even when they are weightless."

"I guess you're right," Margaret said. "I suppose that the second error is using a weightless hammer to drive in a bolt." She began to pace the floor.

"No, that's correct," Einstein said. "The hammer still has inertia. When it hits the bolt it has a force. The bolt in the girder also has inertia to stay in place, and it exerts a force to stop the hammer. That allows the bolt to be driven into place."

"In that case, I know what the second error is," said Margaret. "A workman getting hit with a girder is going to be hurt because of the inertia of the girder and his own inertia."

"That's right." Einstein got up and began to follow Margaret as she paced. "The next error is what happens when a worker's suit is ripped. You said he would blow up because of the pressure in his body. But that's not so. The pressure inside his body is much too weak to cause an explosion. In fact, he might be able to live for half a minute in space before he loses consciousness because of the lack of air and the cold."

"Say, didn't they show that in a movie?" asked Margaret. She sat down.

"Yes," Einstein answered, also sitting down, "in *2001: A Space Odyssey* there was a scene showing one of the Jupiter voyagers living for a few seconds in space. A lot of people thought the scene was impossible, but that's actually what would happen if a space suit got ripped."

"That's only three errors, Einstein." Margaret sprang up again and resumed her pacing. "And there's nothing left. You know that a candle will keep burning if there's enough air in the space station."

"I'm afraid not." Einstein shook his head. "Not if

there's no power and the fans are shut off, so that no air moves in the station. A flame can only burn if carbon dioxide and other waste gases rise upward, as they do on Earth. But the gases are weightless in space, so they don't move away. In a short time the waste gases next to the candle will put out the flame."

"Isn't there any way to keep the candle burning?" Margaret asked.

"Sure," Einstein answered. "You can blow on the candle to keep the waste gases moving away. Or you can move the candle around to get it away from the waste gases."

Margaret stood still. She appeared to be thinking. Then she smiled. "Just a minute, Einstein. I never said that the worker put the candle down. He could easily have been carrying it with him so he could see what he was doing. So the candle keeps burning, and you found only three errors, not four. That means that you have to help me write the script."

"Gobble, gobble," said Einstein.

8

The Indian Head Pennies

It was a warm Saturday in early December, but it seemed like a day in spring. The sun was shining, and an overwintering blue jay made a racket in a nearby tree.

It was definitely a day to get out-of-doors, Einstein thought. I'll ask Dennis if he wants to take a bicycle ride up to Potter's Pond, he said to himself.

Einstein knocked on Dennis's door, went in, and said, "Are you doing anything today? How about taking our bikes up to the pond? We can make sandwiches and have lunch up there."

Dennis was polishing his Indian head pennies at

his desk. The pennies dated back to the beginning of the century, and Dennis was proud of his collection.

Dennis looked up from the coins. "I'm supposed to go over to my friend Larry's house to show him my pennies and to see his coin collection. But that's not till after lunch. I could bicycle up to the pond this morning, eat lunch, and then bicycle back to his house."

"Great," Einstein said. "Let's get going."

Dennis nodded and slipped into a jacket. He placed the pennies in a cardboard holder and slipped the holder into his jacket pocket. "I'm ready," he said.

"I'll make sandwiches and you get the bikes out of the garage," Einstein said. "Meet you in front of the house in five minutes."

The bike trip to Potter's Pond was a leisurely one. Along the way Einstein found a bird's feather and showed it to Dennis.

"Feel how light the feather is," Einstein said. "A feather is light, strong, and a good insulator besides. Birds are warm-blooded, you know. Feathers help keep their body heat from escaping."

"Besides all that, feathers make birds look good," Dennis said.

"Oh, did I ever tell you the story about the feathers on a peacock?" Einstein asked.

"Tell me," said Dennis.

"They make a beautiful *tale*," Einstein said. "Do you get it?"

"I get it," Dennis said, "but I wish I didn't."

"I know a lot of bird stories," Einstein continued. "They're cheepers by the dozen."

Dennis didn't laugh. He tried to hold his nose with his fingers, but nearly fell off his bike. "Einstein," he said, "on a scale of one to ten, I would rate that joke a zero."

By the time the boys got to the pond, they were very hungry. They leaned their bikes against a tree and spread out their jackets to sit on. Then they unwrapped their sandwiches and began to eat.

"Where do the frogs in the pond go in winter?" Dennis asked.

"They hibernate in the mud at the bottom of the pond," said Einstein. "It's a kind of deep sleep," he added.

"How do they know when to hibermate?" Dennis asked.

"Hiber*nate*, not hiber*mate*," Einstein said. "They hibernate when the water temperature falls below a certain point. Frogs are cold-blooded animals, which really means that their body temperature varies with their surroundings. When it gets too cold, they simply go to sleep for the winter."

"Well, before we go to sleep for the winter, let's

start back," said Dennis. "I told Larry I'd be over at his house by three."

The boys put on their jackets, cleaned up their litter, and started home on their bikes. About one hundred feet down the path they saw a boy on a bike coming toward them. When the boy got closer, they saw that it was Herman, Pat's best friend.

"Hello, Herman," Einstein said. "How are tricks?"

"Who's that?" Herman said. "Oh, it's you and your kid brother. I wasn't doing any tricks. I was just riding my bike. Pat's the one who does the tricks."

"Never mind, Herman," said Einstein. "I just meant to say hello, and also good-bye. I'll see you in class on Monday."

Einstein and Dennis began to bicycle away. They passed Herman and went down the path and around the bend. After about five minutes of hard cycling Dennis suddenly slammed on his brakes.

"I think I lost my pennies," he cried out. "Let me look in my pockets." He searched through his jacket and his pants pockets. "They're not here," he said. "They must have fallen out of my jacket when I sat on it back at the pond. Let's go back and look."

The boys started to cycle back. They had just come to the bend in the path when they spotted

Herman standing by his bike. Herman was looking at something in his hand that glittered brightly in the sunlight.

"Herman must have found the coins," Dennis said. "Let's get them back.

"Did you find my pennies?" Dennis called out as he bicycled toward Herman.

Herman glanced up and looked startled. "These aren't your pennies," he said. "They're mine." He put the pennies in his pocket.

"Are they Indian head pennies that you just found near the pond?" Dennis asked. "If you did find them, they're mine."

"I didn't find them near the pond," Herman said. "I—er—just dug them up. I found them under a rock on the bicycle path. They must have been there for a long time."

"You mean you didn't find them in a cardboard holder?" Dennis asked.

"What cardboard holder?" said Herman. "I told you I dug them up just the way they are. They don't have your name on them. You can't prove they're your pennies."

"I think I can," said Einstein.

Can you solve the puzzle: How can Einstein prove that the pennies must be the ones that Dennis lost?

"Take out the pennies and let's look at them," Einstein said.

Herman took the pennies out of his pocket and held them in his palm. There were nine shiny Indian head pennies.

"Do they look like your pennies, Dennis?" asked Einstein.

"I'm sure they are," Dennis answered. "I had nine pennies in the holder. And I always keep them shined up."

"I told you I found them in the ground under a rock," Herman said. "They're not yours."

"You couldn't have found those pennies under a rock," said Einstein. "Copper tarnishes very quickly when left outdoors. A copper penny becomes dark and green in a short time. Those pennies are bright and glittery. They must have been polished just recently. If you'd found them in the ground as you said you did, they would have been dull and tarnished."

"I was just kidding," muttered Herman. He threw the pennies toward Dennis, who bent down to pick them up.

"I wouldn't throw pennies if I were you," Einstein said as Herman rode away. "Only a skunk throws a scent."

9

The Snow Sculpture Contest

The day after the first big snowfall was always a special event at the Sparta Middle School. After lunch, instead of regular classes there would be a snow sculpture contest. Each grade was allowed one entry in the contest. The sculpture had to be completed by three o'clock.

The judging would take place the next morning. A committee of parents and teachers would award prizes to the biggest and to the most beautiful snow sculpture.

This year the first big snowfall came in early December. There was plenty of snow for making snow sculptures, but there was a problem. The weather report called for milder temperatures that night and the next day. The warmer air would certainly melt some of the snow. But finally the decision was made to go ahead with the contest.

Margaret was elected chairperson of the sixth grade snow sculpture committee. Pat grumbled at the word "chairperson," but stopped quickly when Margaret asked if he wanted to make something of it.

"Class," Margaret said, "this year the sixth grade is going to win both prizes for the first time. Usually the eighth grade wins the prize for the biggest sculpture, because they have the biggest kids collecting the snow. But this year our sixth grade is going to beat them by working harder. So let's get out there after lunch and work, work, work!"

The contest began promptly at one o'clock. The snow was soft and fluffy, easy to pack and just right for making a snow sculpture. At first everyone worked quickly, and huge amounts of snow were collected. The sculpture grew and grew. But as time went on, the sixth graders began to get tired and they slowed down. The snow began to melt as the air temperature rose.

Einstein dumped a load of snow that he had collected and looked at Margaret. "I don't know if we're going to beat the eighth grade," he said. "I just took a look at their sculpture, and it's bigger than ours. The seventh grade's is smaller than ours and no contest."

"How much bigger *is* the eighth grade's sculpture, Einstein?"

"Not that much," Einstein admitted. "But those kids are still working, and our class has slowed down a lot."

"Well, think of something, Einstein Anderson!" Margaret exclaimed. "How about using science to help us?"

"Now wait a minute, Margaret," said Einstein. "You know we're not supposed to use any tools for building a snow sculpture."

"I'm not talking about using tools," Margaret said. "I'm talking about using our brains."

"Sure," said Einstein. "I'm trying to think, but I'm so cold, wet, and tired that it's not that easy. And I fell down and hurt my ankle besides."

"I'm sorry, Einstein," Margaret said. "I hope your ankle is O.K."

"I suppose it is," Einstein replied. Then his face brightened. "Say," he said, "do you know what often falls but never gets hurt?"

"What?" Margaret asked.

"Snow," said Einstein.

"Get back to work," Margaret said.

"Right, chairperson," Einstein said.

It was just ten minutes before three when Margaret came up to speak to Einstein. "I'm worried about our winning," she said. "I think we would win for most beautiful snow sculpture if they judged now. But the snow is sure to melt overnight, and who knows what our sculpture will look like in the morning." She tried to smile but just looked more concerned.

"How about the prize for the largest one?" asked Einstein. "Have you compared ours to the eighth grade's?"

"That's about a toss-up," said Margaret. "The way things are going, we may win neither prize in-

stead of both. I really feel bad. Isn't there anything you can think of to do, Einstein?"

Einstein was quiet for a few minutes. Then he pushed back his glasses, which were slipping down, and said, "I have an idea. Let's get some of those old blankets that are in the storeroom."

"I don't think that keeping warm is going to help us win," Margaret said.

"Keeping warm is not the only use for a blanket," said Einstein.

Can you solve the puzzle: How does Einstein plan to use blankets to help his class win the snow sculpture contest?

"I hope you know what you're doing." Margaret sighed. "I'll get some of the class to help you carry the blankets."

In a short time the boys and girls came back laden with blankets.

"O.K.," Einstein said. "Let's start wrapping the snow sculpture in the blankets. Two layers of blankets should be enough."

"Are you crazy?" Pat asked. "If we wrap the sculpture, it will be all melted by tomorrow. We want to keep the snow cold, not warm!"

"That's exactly what the blankets will do," Einstein answered. "Blankets contain layers of air pockets just like clothing. The air is trapped in the mesh of the wool or whatever fabric you use. When air is trapped in that way, it can't transmit heat."

"But we want to keep the cold in," said Pat.

"Blankets do that by preventing heat from getting through the trapped air to the snow inside. Two blankets will have more trapped air spaces, so a double blanket will be an even better insulator."

"I hope it works, Einstein," Margaret said. "If our sculpture doesn't melt, we're sure to win at least one prize."

"We will," said Einstein. "A long time ago people used to cut up blocks of ice in winter and keep them for use in the summer. The trick in keeping the ice from melting was to use an insulator with many air pockets. Some people would cover the ice with layers of sawdust. Others would use old blankets."

"But how do you know that it will work now?" Pat asked. "Just because it worked a long time ago?"

"That's the beauty of science," explained Einstein. "Once you understand how something works, you can use that understanding to make it work again and again."

"I'm sorry I doubted you," Margaret said.

"Science means that you never have to say you're sorry," said Einstein.

"Ugh," Margaret said, but she smiled broadly.

"But saying ugh is O.K.," said Einstein with an answering grin.

10

The Sleigh Race

It turned much colder a few days after the snow sculpture contest. Einstein's solution to the puzzle of the melting snow had helped his sixth grade class win both prizes in the contest, much to the dismay of the seventh and eighth graders. They vowed to beat the sixth graders in a contest at the winter carnival, regardless of what Einstein did.

The winter carnival was held just before school closed for the Christmas holidays. Depending on the weather, there would be all sorts of contests, games, and entertainments.

The first part of the carnival was held indoors.

Each of the grades presented a program to the rest of the school. There was also a school sing and a great lunch of hamburgers, pizza, and ice cream.

After lunch the entire school went out to a nearby park for winter games. The cold weather had frozen the water in Potter's Pond so that it could be used for skating. There was also plenty of snow around for sleighing, tumbling in the drifts, and more snow sculpture building. There was supposed to be no snowball throwing, but every once in a while someone would pitch one at a tree or a nearby friend.

Einstein was skating on the pond, along with Margaret and some of his sixth grade classmates, when a group of seventh graders called them over.

"The seventh grade challenges the sixth grade to a tug of war," said one of the seventh graders. "Our whole class against your whole class."

"That's not a very fair contest," Einstein said. "First of all, you weigh more than we do, and second of all, there are more seventh graders than sixth graders."

"What are you? Chicken?" the seventh grader said.

"You're the one who's trying to egg me on," Einstein said.

"Come on, Einstein," the seventh grader said

impatiently. "If you don't want to have a tug of war, then name the contest. We'll beat you in anything you say."

"Don't be so sure," Einstein said. "This was the first year the sixth grade won in the snow sculpture contest."

"Let's make a bet on the contest, Einstein," said another seventh grader. "The losers have to bow down to the winners every time they pass them in the halls at school."

"O.K.," said Einstein, "you're on. But we get to name the contest."

"But we got to agree to it," said the seventh grader.

"Right," Einstein said. "Our class will meet your class back here in ten minutes, and then we'll decide on the contest."

The seventh graders went off to get the rest of their classmates. Einstein's classmates gathered around him silently. They seemed glum.

Finally Margaret spoke up. "Einstein, I think you shouldn't have bet them on the contest. They're not going to agree to anything they can't win. And if they win, we're going to have to bow down to them in school. It's embarrassing."

"I know," said Einstein. "Let me think for a minute."

After a few minutes Einstein pushed his glasses back on his nose and said, "I have an idea for a sleigh race that I think will work."

"A sleigh race doesn't sound too good," Margaret said. "The seventh graders are bigger and faster than we are."

"But this is a special kind of sleigh race," Einstein said. "Let's get the rest of our class together and see what happens."

Ten minutes later all the sixth and the seventh

graders were clustered together. Many eighth graders were also in the crowd, watching to see what would happen.

"Are you ready to lose?" asked one of the seventh graders. "What kind of a race do you want us to beat you at?"

"How about a sleigh race?" Einstein said. "A special kind of sleigh race," he added.

"What kind?" the seventh grader asked.

"Pulling a loaded sleigh a distance of one hundred yards," Einstein said. "Two kids will sit on the sleigh and two kids will pull. Whoever crosses the finish line first wins."

"That sounds O.K.," said the leader of the seventh graders. "But what's so special about that race?"

"Here's the special part," said Einstein. "We're so sure we're going to beat you that we're going to start ten yards behind the starting line."

"You're crazy," said the seventh grader. "We'll beat you easily."

"Maybe you're right," said Einstein. "Ten yards is a big handicap. Suppose you let us start pulling and wait until we're two yards behind the starting line. Then you can start pulling."

"But we'll still be ahead of you by two yards," said the sixth grader.

Einstein smiled. "Are you chickening out?" he asked.

"Let's go," said the seventh grader. "I hope you know how to bow down."

Can you solve the puzzle: How can Einstein expect to win a race in which his team starts two yards behind?

"Are you sure you know what you're doing, Einstein?" Margaret asked. "What's all that business about starting ten yards behind and then letting them start when we're two yards behind?"

"That's why we're going to win," Einstein said. "You'll see."

Einstein quickly selected the two lightest kids in the sixth grade to sit on the sleigh and the two fastest kids to pull the sleigh.

In a few minutes the race began. It was no contest. The sixth grade sleigh passed the seventh grade sleigh easily and was yards ahead at the finish line. The sixth graders cheered wildly. The seventh graders just looked disgusted. "That's the last time we'll let Einstein Anderson set the rules for a race," one seventh grader said.

After the crowd broke up and the children went back to their games, an excited Margaret drew Einstein aside. "Explain why we won," she said. "I couldn't believe it was so easy."

"It's all because of inertia," Einstein said. "Inertia is a force that acts to keep an object at rest or to keep it in motion. In other words, an object tries to keep doing what it is doing. A sleigh has a lot of inertia when it's at rest. You need a lot of force to get it moving. But once the sleigh is in action, inertia keeps it moving. Then all you have to do is run as fast as you can."

"But both sleighs had the same amount of inertia," said Margaret.

"But we started pulling earlier," said Einstein. "By the time the seventh graders started to pull, we were going at full speed. We shot past them almost at the starting line. In a short race of a hundred yards they had no chance to catch up. We were yards ahead by the time they got going."

"I'm proud of you," Margaret said. "The seventh grade doesn't have a chance to win when you start thinking."

"I'm a real hard-boiled egg," Einstein said.

"Why are you a hard-boiled egg?" Margaret asked in a puzzled way.

"You know that a hard-boiled egg is tough to beat," said Einstein.

"That's terrible," Margaret said with a laugh. "I hope that's the last egg joke I hear today."

"Eggs-actly," said Einstein. "Eggs-cuse me."

ABOUT THE AUTHOR

SEYMOUR SIMON is one of America's leading science writers for young readers. Mr. Simon has written more than sixty books, among which are *The Secret Clocks*, *Look to the Night Sky*, *The Paper Airplane Book*, and *Pets in a Jar*, all for Viking.

For many years Mr. Simon was a science teacher in junior high school. He lives on Long Island.

D